Clothes Long Ago

Written by Tracey Michele

Picture Dictionary

dress

jacket

nightgowns

Read the
picture dictionary.
You will find these words
in the book.

straw hats

swimsuits

top hat

This girl wore a dress
to the park long ago.
What else did she wear?

hat
petticoat

Boys wore straw hats
to school long ago.
What else did they wear?

tie
coat
FIRST

Children wore wool swimsuits to the beach long ago. What else did they wear to the beach?

suspenders
belt

What did men wear
at work long ago?
This man wore a jacket.
What else did he wear?

shirt
vest

Long ago,
girls wore nightgowns
to bed.
What else did they wear?

nightcap
bed socks

What did men wear
out at night long ago?
This man wore a top hat.
What else did he wear?

handkerchief
gloves

Activity Page

1. Choose one of the photos in the book.
2. Write a story about the photo. Use these words in your story:
   they to the

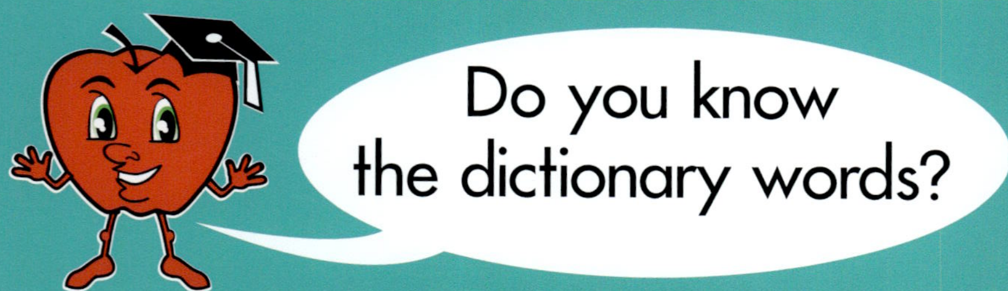